VERENE SARTER

By the Grace of Extinction

She Chooses Death

Contents

1

Chapter One

Humanity is gone. We ran out of time. We all came together in the end, all inequalities eradicated, but we didn't face the climate crisis before the point of no return. Just not enough profit.

But as a collective parting gift to the remaining life on Earth, we used our technology to push the Earth out of the Sun's orbit saving it from the death of the star which would have consumed the planet in its expansion. And that's all that's left of us, traces of our technology and infrastructure, scattered around and reclaimed by the Earth and its life.

That's when we are now; six billion years in the future. And there's new life, new humanoid species; each largely unaware of the other. These peoples are connected to nature, they are bound to it. They cannot mistake, ignore or misinterpret nature's messages. The cause of their demise could never be the same as ours. They will take their last breaths for another reason.

Their societies are riddled with imperfections, the kinds of which we solved just as we departed. Nature is not the beast they are fighting, but nurture. These imperfections could have them wipe themselves out.

There is a revolutionary spirit in the air, an aura of change just as there had been for humanity's last days on Earth; another cataclysm on the brink of genesis, this too starting with a symptom.

The biofluorescent crystal phoenix encrusted into the dome of the sky emits sunlight, collected and dispersed from the death of the star.

The sunlight can be seen through, and the phoenix visible in times of great change… if conscience calls you to look up. The phoenix may follow you in some way to demand your acceptance of the inevitable. Confronting it is another matter. But these people would know what was coming… if they just looked up.

These people, a species resembling what would be considered salamanders, are about to discover the symptom.

"I hope the Elders can help. I've never heard of anything like this before," the woman said.

"It will be fine, sweetheart. The Elders know all," her partner said.

The well-dressed couple continued on their way,

hand-in-hand, in silence, for the rest of the walk up to Elders Hill. There they would receive counsel about this most unusual of situations.

When the couple got to the top of Elders Hill, they were greeted by one of the men of the Council.

"Hello there. What brings you to us on this fine day?" The Elder asked.

"I... we... she didn't fall pregnant," the man said.

The woman looked offended but said nothing.

A series of emotions passed behind the Elder's eyes.

"I'm sure all will be fine. Just try again," the Elder said.

"Ah... Ok. We will. Come on sweetheart," the man said, attempting to put his arm around his partner.

She shrugged him off, and walked away in silence, with her arms crossed, back down the hill. Her partner followed.

The Elder watched the couple get smaller as they walked back to the village in the pond. When he was sure they were out of earshot he yelled for a guard to call to the rest of the Council. There needed to be a meeting.

The Elder went back inside to the Meeting Hall where the rest of the men were waiting for him.

"Why are we here Lithinel?" A man asked.

"I bring grave news to you. An esteemed couple approached me while I was out on the hill. They told me they failed to conceive," Lithinel said.

There was silence.

"What do we say our plan is? I say we call for the spirit worker," Lithinel said.

"I don't think it would be wise to be involved with such a person as that spirit worker, Lithinel. How can we be sure we can control him, after what he attempted last time we got him involved?" The Elder from before stated. The men refrained from laughing at the shaman, as they were reminded of the shaman's antics.

"Don't you think if we knew what to do, that there would be no need to call a meeting? How many times have you known for a respectable couple or partnership to be infertile?" Lithinel said.

"This is beyond our expertise. It is clear we need outside help, even if that means receiving it from unsavoury, disruptive types like that shaman," Lithinel said. He looked around the Hall, seeing all heads begrudgingly nodding.

"Excellent. I'm glad we're all in agreement. I will have someone send for the shaman tomorrow," Lithinel said.

2

Chapter Two

U nder the stars, the glint of the phoenix's jewelled eyes, two friends, both humanoid, one a chameleon, the other a salamander, lay upon a grassy knoll.

"The stars are burning brightly tonight. Look at those two," Iaina said breathlessly.

"You sound like you're about to fall asleep, don't make me carry you back to the pond entrance," Zirr said.

"Don't fuss, I'm just really relaxed," Iaina said.

"You shouldn't be this relaxed from merely lying on a hill. Your duties are crushing you, aren't they?" Zirr asked.

"I don't understand why you help that village, after what happened last time," Zirr said.

"What do you mean?" Iaina asked.

"You do your duty as a shaman, you're at the beck

and call of Lithinel, you give them everything, solve their problems. They give absolutely nothing," Zirr said.

"You're overreacting. Besides, it's in the job description," Iaina said.

Zirr gave Iaina a sideways look with raised eyebrows.

"Uh huh," Zirr said.

Iaina sat up to shoot Zirr a filthy look. He wasn't there, however. Or at least she figured he wasn't. She couldn't be sure because he was a chameleon, and he loved camouflaging himself whenever he pissed off Iaina. She tapped the ground where he had been.

"Ow," Zirr said.

"Still here, are we? If you're going to disturb my rest, please leave," Iaina said.

Zirr turned his camouflage off and stayed quiet.

"You're wrong about the village," Iaina's voice trailed off.

Iaina laid down completely, resting her head on her interlacing fingers. Zirr sat up on his elbows and watched Iaina out of the corner of his eye. His fear had come true. She had fallen asleep.

Damn you woman.

3

Chapter Three

L*et's see what's going on around the village.*
Behind closed doors, a little boy is having a tantrum because he is overwhelmed. He is kicking and stomping at the ground while seated. He is covering his ears and crying because he just wants the sound of his parents fighting to stop.

"Look what you did! You made him cry!" His mother said.

"How dare you speak to me like that!" The father said.

Instead of taking his rage out on his wife physically, it hadn't escalated to that. Yet. He took it out on his son. He dragged the little boy by his arm into his bedroom and restrained him by putting his shirt above his head, behind his neck. He is lying face down on his bed. He is too little to fix his shirt himself.

Across the road, an old woman's garden. The old woman knelt in the garden tending to her flowers. She screwed her face up as a teenage girl walked past wearing a shorter robe than what was custom. She transferred the look of disapproval to the flowers by turning her gaze back down to them. Maybe she would have felt differently if she had known the girl was feeling confident for the first time in her body and was allowing herself to gain weight, and was no longer ashamed of the cut marks between her legs. But that's doubtful.

That's what I thought.

"Mummy, I have a crush," a little girl said.

"Ooh, what's his name?" Her mother asked.

The little girl went tight-lipped and looked away from her mother. She was searching for an acceptable answer.

"I like Banan," the little girl said.

That was when she learned to hide how she really felt. Her crush was actually on a girl. The little girl would continue to isolate herself from her mother. She would tell her nothing. If the natural course of events were to unfold, given time, she would cut her mother out of her life completely when she was old enough. The mother would have no idea why.

A group of young men sit in a circle bragging about their sexual exploits.

"She wasn't budging, but I kept touching her. Then

she gave it to me," one man said.

"She must have wanted it so badly," another man said. They fist-bump.

They did not have the self-awareness to realise they were enforcing the training little girls undergo to become compliant, docile women. Or that women will cave to being coerced, to reclaim a sense of power when worn down enough. They cannot read women. That is not what desire looks like.

In the community supply store, a woman is being dragged through by her boyfriend. In public. She is whimpering and cowering. Her voice gives away her fear. Everyone has turned away. They dare not look. Or they might just realise their cowardice as they stand there doing nothing. If one of them was to snap out of the spell the emboldened boyfriend had cast on them, they would be able to feel just how hard everyone else *isn't* looking. If they can pretend it isn't happening, the bully doesn't exist. It isn't right for them to intervene in another's business, anyway. Pay no mind to the fact it's in public.

I told her so. She'll find out soon enough.

He uncrossed his legs and returned to the fire by the waterfall.

4

Chapter Four

L ithinel waited for the messenger to appear from over the hill. He paced back and forth, growing agitated the longer he had to wait. He decided he had had enough. He would go get him himself. Lithinel headed down the hill into the network of ponds and went straight to the messenger's house.

On his way there, he went over in his mind the severity of the situation. He looked down at children playing around their parents. What if that stopped? If that 'supply' dried up? If the population didn't replace and sustain itself?

He got to the messenger's house. He knocked on the door. Muffled noises, but no discernible response. The noises continued. Lithinel figured he just couldn't be heard. He needed to get closer.

Lithinel entered the house of the messenger and went to the bedroom. He opened the door. He saw the back of the messenger. He had his pants around his ankles and a set of legs open before him.

"Kylel! Get your clothes on!" Lithinel said through gritted teeth.

"Oh hi Dad," Kylel said.

"When I gave this task to you, I thought you understood how serious this is," Lithinel said.

Kylel pulled his pants up. The woman who had been lying beneath him had froze and looked stunned, her expression was blank. Kylel got off her and her blinking returned to normal. She looked around confused. She looked down at her body and pulled her robe back into place. She got off the bed gingerly and without making eye contact with either of the men, walked briskly out the house and tried to remain unseen as she walked through the pond network to her home. Lithinel took in that woman's body language.

Kylel turned around to answer his father. He hadn't paid that woman or her exit any attention.

"Why would I care if the women can't have children? That just works better for me," Kylel said.

"Because you are going to join the Council one day. And have your own children!" Lithinel said.

"Get dressed. Eat something, then leave immediately for the spirit worker's shack," Lithinel said.

Kylel dragged his feet in following his father's instructions. He zoned out. Lithinel saw him finish eating.

"Are you ready to go get the spirit worker?" Lithinel asked.

"Yes father, I am," Kylel said.

"Good. Go!" Lithinel said. He left his son's house after him.

Kylel wandered over grassy hills on his way to the shaman's home, getting lost occasionally as he misremembered his father's directions, and other times getting lost in memories of women. He had never been particularly good at taking orders, or staying focused. He didn't fully grasp the severity of the situation.

Lithinel knew this and it made him worry. If Kylel didn't show natural promise to join the Council, how could the other elders be bribed when there's no avenue in a horizontal power structure?

Kylel meandered back onto the correct path. He looked ahead, and realised he was close. He had failed to navigate his way to the spirit worker, but had succeeded in getting there nonetheless.

Kylel came as close as he could to thinking it was a good idea to not go off the path anymore. He walked on the path and stayed there. After some minutes he found himself at the edge of a large pond. Peering into the water he could see a small shack. He figured this must be where the shaman lives. He got into the water and walked down the stairs to the home.

The shack gave off an aura of peace and reigned-in power, with an air of understanding. Fish swam by freely, fearing nothing, not even their death at the hands of the shaman when they would ask them to die to sustain them. Kylel became so mesmerised by the inhabitants of the pond he had almost completely forgotten about their steward; the reason he was there.

The errand boy finally snapped out of it and walked up to the front door. Before he could knock, he heard a distinct yet distorted voice from within the dwelling call to him.

"The door's open. You may come in," beckoned the voice of the shaman.

Kylel made his way inside, searching through a few rooms, but not finding the shaman until reaching the kitchen. When he got there, he found a woman wearing modest, loose flowing robes of an aqua tint, which gently contrasted her mousy brown hair. She was turned away from him, working on a preparation for some ritual or journey. After taking the shaman in for a few moments, Kylel decided to speak.

"I've been sent by my father, Lithinel, to inform you of a problem back in the village," Kylel said somewhat tense.

"What's the problem?" The spirit worker asked. She still hadn't turned around.

"There's infertility throughout the whole village," he said.

"Wow. Normally that's due to a birth defect or injury to the reproductive system. That can't be the cause for all the villagers," she said.

"I understand why you've come," she said.

"What is your name by the way?" He asked.

"Oh, Iaina. I knew your father back in the day. And yours…?" Iaina continued working on her concoction.

"Kylel. Oh wow… really? How did you know him?" Kylel asked.

She bent over to pick up a small pot. Kylel admired what he could of the shaman's body, while her robes clung to her outline.

"We used to be family friends… but then we grew apart," Iaina said.

"Why did you grow apart?" Kylel asked.

"We grew into different people. He settled down, and had you, apparently," Iaina said.

"Ha. Do you have children?" Kylel asked.

"No, it wasn't meant to be," Iaina said.

Kylel peered up and down over Iaina's body with a darkened expression. He had removed at least one layer of her clothing in his mind, at this point. He certainly would have liked to remove some of his own. His pants were becoming uncomfortably tight.

"I'm sure there's still time," Kylel said huskily.

"Aha, I don't know about that. From what you've told me it sounds like I might have a hard time," Iaina said, laughing easily. She was beginning to relax into Kylel's presence. Kylel chuckled heartily. He enjoyed her wit.

"Very true," Kylel said.

"Could you pass me that herb there?" Iaina gestured to her herb rack.

"Sure," Kylel reached for the herb and handed it to Iaina. He couldn't look away from her hand. Iaina noticed he had gone quiet.

"Is something wrong?" Iaina asked. She turned around.

The sight of Iaina's skin registered in Kylel's mind. It took a few moments for the colour to sink in. It was deeper than Kylel was anticipating. It was the colour one would expect of a male-bodied member of their species. Kylel had that same colour. Before Iaina could recognise her egregious error, Kylel had bent her over her work bench and twisted her left arm. Kylel used his weight to bear down on Iaina; she was also restrained by his right hand.

"Are you trying to trick me?!" Kylel screamed into Iaina's ear.

"Please don't hurt me," Iaina begged.

Kylel started to reach under Iaina's robes with his left hand to confirm his fear. Iaina felt Kylel grope her while she thrashed about and struggled to

15

breathe, the weight of the messenger restricting her breathing as it did her movement. Iaina eventually succumbed to stillness. Iaina's mind panicked as she felt the likelihood of her surviving this encounter slip away. As the shaman began to recall memories from her life, she wondered who would succeed her in her role as the caretaker of all things wild and beautiful.

"So you think you're a woman, hey?! I can't believe you would do this to me! How dare you make me lust for you! You're disgusting, you know that?!" Kylel said.

Iaina went deeper into an altered state.

"Please... Just let me live... I won't tell anyone about this, I promise," Iaina said.

"You've got that right bitch!" Kylel howled at the fading shaman.

Kylel persisted in his attacks, as he paired his verbal blows now with brute physicality. He grabbed the shaman by her hair and began repeatedly slamming her head down into her once-beloved counter.

"You..." Iaina started.

"What's that?!" Kylel asked indignantly.

"...sent by... " Iaina said.

"Fuck!" Kylel said.

In letting his rage and disgust take over him, Kylel had forgotten why he was in the shaman's home in the first place. He began pacing and mumbling in his own reality, a little over a metre away from her. Even though Iaina had nearly been asphyxiated to the point of unconsciousness, her state had begun returning to normal. As she came back to her senses, she was ever-aware of her abuser's presence and position. Iaina peeled herself off her work bench, as she finally felt able to move once more.

Kylel was still pacing agitated and muttering to himself.

"Kylel; I know; you know... that we have to work together," Iaina said swallowing her nerves in intervals.

Kylel had stopped to glare at his victim. Iaina watched something behind his eyes flash. After this encounter, she would recognise that sight as the moment he decided to do what he did next.

Iaina blinked, and in that second, Kylel was once again on top of her. This time was different however, as he wasn't constraining her breath with his weight, but with his hands. He was now strangling her. He wanted to watch the life drain from her eyes.

Just as he had a firm grasp of her neck with both hands, a massive shadow appeared at the edge of Iaina's much-dimmed periphery. She had successfully summoned a beast.

The sight of the gargantuan fish which was twice the length of Kylel's height could easily have ended his life in one decisive bite. His head and neck disappearing clean-off within a second. Kylel understood this well. He ran out of the shaman's dwelling shrieking. Iaina dealt with the mental and emotional exhaustion which the violence had meted out. She worked on healing herself from this encounter.

She slumped to the floor and sat against the counter's doors. She thanked the fish she summoned, and it returned to its school.

"Well… he obviously wasn't told about me then, was he?" She said to no one.

Iaina continued to sit down on the ground, rubbing her throat and face, and checking her arm for injury. She felt she needed to keep moving it to help the pain dissipate. She sat there lost in her thoughts. She moved her hand to the back of her head, thinking. She inhaled sharply.

"Ah," she pulled her hand back. There was blood coming from where Kylel had grabbed her hair.

A necklace Iaina wore everyday did something it hadn't for a long time. It resembled a phoenix, and it seared against her neck.

"Mhm," she said, from the pain.

She sat there in the quietness, on the ground looking around her home, remembering everything that had happened there. She nodded and sighed in acceptance. The necklace finally calmed.

"Wow," she said.

Chapter Five

I guess I have a duty to investigate.

The phoenix necklace gave Iaina a light searing. *Shush you.*

Iaina headed up the stairs to leave her pond. She walked across the grass, down the stairs into the network of ponds.

"I guess it makes sense to ask around," Iaina said.

Iaina stood at the centre of the village, houses sprawling out all around her. Where to start?

Start at one tip of the village, work my way to the other end.

Iaina turned to her left to start at that end. She knocked on the door. She hadn't thought about what she was going to say beforehand. Time to test her improv skills. The door opened to an old man.

"Hi, I'm the shaman. I was wondering if I may ask you a few questions," Iaina said.

The elderly man clutched the door to his side with a vice grip and held it in a position reminiscent of someone wielding a sword, ready to charge. He didn't speak, he only gave her a quietly horrified look. She calmly held his gaze. She wasn't easily put off.

"Perhaps I'll come back at another time," Iaina said. She smiled in a smug manner.

The elderly man almost slammed the door shut in her face, but the urge to make sure she was gone was too strong. He held the door open an inch and peaked out from behind it to watch her go.

Fair enough, asshole.

Iaina walked to the house next door and repeated the process. This time a little girl opened the door and called for her parents.

"Mummy, there's a weirdo here," the little girl said.

Her mother came out from the kitchen.

"Honey, that isn't very nice. Say sorry," the mother said.

Iaina came into view as she approached her front door. She raised her eyebrows.

"Hi," the mother said tensely.

"Hi," Iaina said.

"Right, so um… can I ask you what you know about the infertility crisis?" Iaina asked.

The mother swallowed, wrung her hands together, and looked away. But ultimately nodded.

"Sure," the mother said. She shrugged her shoulders.

"Clearly you haven't struggled to fall pregnant… unless. Have you? Have you been trying for another?" Iaina asked.

She looked uncomfortable.

"I don't think I can answer that," the mother said.

"Sorry. Can you tell me about anyone you know who's struggling to fall pregnant?" Iaina asked.

The mother nodded.

"I've heard about it. It's usually an injury of some type. I think my friend's cousin or somebody like that has gone through it," the mother said.

"And how did she deal with it?" Iaina asked.

"Her husband left her because she wouldn't stop miscarrying," the mother said.

Iaina casually glanced into the woman's face and saw tears about to spill out of her eyes.

"Ok, I think you've been very helpful. Thank you," Iaina said.

The mother pulled her daughter back inside and hastily closed the door.

Iaina inhaled and exhaled deeply and let her shoulders fall nice and relaxed. She needed to de-stress.

She turned away from the house. She decided a little stroll would help her digest what just happened. She skipped over a few streets. Nothing would be

21

gained by asking literally everyone. But she had something to lose by doing that. Energy definitely. Time too, probably.

Iaina walked awhile then stopped out front a well-maintained, but heritage house. She hadn't seen too many houses like it before, and this one stood out for the energy she received from it. It was peaceful. Relaxed. She approached and knocked as she had done.

A charming elderly woman answered the door. She was beaming. Iaina could hear a group in the living room.

"Have I come at a bad time?" Iaina asked.

The elderly woman waved Iaina inside.

"No dear, come in," she said.

"Oh wow, ok," Iaina said. The elderly woman got behind Iaina and practically shoved her inside.

Once inside, Iaina saw elderly couples sitting together in the living room holding hands. Iaina stood in the centre, on display. She held onto her left wrist as a comfortable standing position.

"What was it that you wanted dear?" the woman of the house asked. She was also standing.

"What have you heard of the infertility crisis?" Iaina asked.

All the people went quiet and their expressions turned solemn, except for Iaina. She was waiting for answers.

"I don't remember anything like this happening before," a seated woman said.

"There's something different about the women today. They've changed," her husband chimed in.

The woman of the house approached the middle of the circle, towards Iaina. She spoke to the man.

"There have always been people with difficulties," she said.

"I don't know about that. I don't remember it," he said.

"Injury or birth defect," the woman of the house suggested.

The man crossed his arms in a sulk and looked at Iaina in disgust.

"I don't care. If you can't get pregnant, you're not a real woman," he said.

Iaina felt that. She clutched her wrist tight to soothe herself. Only the woman who owned the house, who had greeted her had any sympathy. The rest of the husbands and wives nodded in unison.

"And some of the things parents let their children do these days. It's unthinkable," his wife said.

"Like what?" Iaina asked.

"They don't get enough guidance. They need tough love," the seated woman said.

Iaina could hear what she was really saying. The others could too… only they agreed. They were still nodding. The woman was still talking but Iaina had zoned out after "tough love".

Children being themselves... the horror.

Iaina imagined herself holding her hand up to her mouth to gasp in shock. She accidentally nearly did it. She stopped herself in time before the others could see. She didn't need them to ask her what was wrong, and for her to explain *that entire scenario.* She snickered at that thought quietly.

Iaina made eye contact with the woman of the house. She headed to the door to see Iaina out.

"I'm so sorry about that. I didn't know my friends were like that," she said.

"It's fine," Iaina said.

"No it isn't. I had a friend like you when I was very young. If things had been different…" She said.

"When I opened the door and saw you, I saw her…" She said.

Her face betrayed memories of pain, anguish and regret. She looked solemn as she stared at the floor.

"What happened to her?" Iaina asked.

She raised her eyes to show Iaina they were about to spill over. Iaina returned the solemnity and whispered.

"Thank you," Iaina said. The necklace simmered.

Iaina left the kindly woman's house and continued on her way to the other end of the village.

Iaina had been walking in the middle of the street. She was enjoying her little outing. She hadn't been to every part of the village and was taking her time sight-seeing. Noticing the difference in architecture, the choices in landscaping. She felt carefree despite how today's task had gone so far. That was about to change.

Kylel came walking down the street on Iaina's left. He had seen her before she had seen him. He walked with an exaggerated swagger like he was trying to make himself seem bigger. He stared her down and did not let up, but did not approach to touch her either. He had not forgotten her though. He looked her up and down as he had in her shack. She visibly trembled. He smirked and finally picked up the pace. She had given him what he wanted. This time.

Iaina felt herself stumble and jolt from her encounter with Kylel in the street. Her breathing was rapid and shallow. But she had always been good at calming herself down. She had had to figure out many coping strategies over the years. She bent over maintaining the natural curve of her back and held onto her waist. She took deep breaths. This position allowed her torso to open up. She did this until she had relaxed enough to continue.

She straightened and kept walking. Iaina made it to the very other end of the village. There was a lone house. It stood apart from the rest of the village as it was cloistered away in it's own pond. All the other houses where situated in interconnecting ponds. This one was in a cave almost. The current was different. Light didn't reach here quite so easily.

Iaina began the approach to the house very slowly. She didn't know if it was inhabited. She came up to the window and saw a woman in her early thirties inside. She was facing side on to Iaina, but Iaina could distinctly see her face.

"Excuse me. Can we have a little talk?" Iaina asked.

The woman startled and dropped what she had been holding in her hands. Luckily she was working on a bench. The bench caught it.

Why did I just do that?

Iaina was not enjoying watching her social skills deteriorate before her eyes.

The woman braced against the bench and exhaled deeply, pursing her lips, attempting to calm herself. She arched her back slightly and tilted her head back.

"And what would you like to talk about?" She asked.

"The infertility crisis," Iaina said.

The woman let her head roll forward in thought. Whatever the significance of Iaina's statement was, she wasn't about to divulge it quickly or without serious consideration first. She pushed off from the bench and headed around to the front door. Iaina saw where she was headed and followed.

"Come in," she said.

Iaina stepped in and noticed she had the setup of a

herbalist. She would be asked for help more so than Iaina.

"Have you been around the village asking?" She asked.

"Yes, it seemed wise to investigate," Iaina said.

"Has anyone been honest with you?" She asked.

"They've given reasons like injury or birth defect. I understand 'birth defect' but…," Iaina said.

"Injury means a few things. The women aren't always emotionally ready for pregnancy. Their minds shut down any possibility of falling pregnant. Their living situations may be dangerous, they may be undernourished. These are simple fixes," she said.

The woman hesitated with the next part. She was admiring the floor and fidgeting with a scroll.

"Sometimes… it's more serious. Husbands are too rough with their wives. Women are left infertile from being…" She said.

"Raped," Iaina said.

"Yes," she said.

"Makes you wonder if all the 'birth defects' are really 'birth defects', or just 'injuries' at a younger age," Iaina said.

A smothering silence suffocated the room. The gravity of the realisation wore the two women down. A dark cloud had moved in over the house. They both looked despondently at the floor. Iaina broke the silence. She gazed up slowly, still in a low mood.

"Thank you for your time. You have been most helpful…" Iaina said.

She leaned in, to prompt the woman. The woman cleared her throat and blinked rapidly.

"Ah, Caasa," Caasa said.

"Thank you Caasa. I appreciate you being… willing to talk with me," Iaina said.

"You bear witness to other people's pain. Handling the trauma of others takes a lot, you really know how to take care of yourself," Iaina said.

6

Chapter Six

C aasa was covered in dust. It was all over her smock and face. Her nose got the worst of it. She had been sweeping the stairs of the Council building on Elder's Hill for an hour. Brushing the dirt and dust into her face made her cough and sweat. The sweat dripping down her nose was relentless; she couldn't stop wiping it away.

She sat down on one of the steps she just cleaned to take a break. From where she was, she could hear children playing outside. She wished she didn't have to do chores, and that she could play with them. She figured no one would notice if she played for five minutes.

Caasa whipped the children's butts, being 15, and them being around 8 years old. Having the physical advantage felt incredible; she just kept winning, round after round. Her break had been longer than five minutes. The more she won, the louder her victorious cheers got. She had drawn the attention of a young man in his late teens. She thought of him as an acquaintance. He came into view.

"Oh, hi Kylel," Caasa said.

Caasa kept playing while Kylel just watched. He stood there, eyeing her every move, every turn of her hips, every lunge for the ball. She ignored him, and the strange expression on his face.

"So what are you doing later?" Kylel asked.

"What?" she asked.

"Damn," she said, missing the ball.

"I said 'what are you doing later?'" Kylel said.

Caasa stopped the game at Kylel's question. It was getting dark, and she hadn't realised it.

"Crap," she said.

She ran back inside to finish what should have been completed half an hour ago. Afterwards, she came rushing out, down the hill. She was expected back home to help prepare dinner. Luckily, there was still plenty of daylight left.

"Bye," she said.

"Where are you going?" he asked.

"Home," she said.

He followed after her down the hill, to the pond network. Caasa looked startled at Kylel's continued presence. They descended the stairs together. Caasa headed home, with Kylel still following.

"So how's your father?" she asked, folding her arms in front of her.

"He's good. Always busy. He complains about the other Council members though," he said.

"That sucks," she said.

"Anyway, my house is here," she said, rubbing the back of her neck.

"See you tomorrow," he said.

"Huh, yeah," she said.

Kylel walked away. Caasa exhaled. She turned towards her front door, and smiled at the familiar face. He stepped forward and kissed a clean patch on her cheek.

"So are you going to see him tomorrow?" her boyfriend Jaxon asked.

She punched him.

"Ow," he said.

"I don't know why he's been acting like that recently," she said.

"Yeah, it is weird. Just remember you're my girlfriend," he said.

Caasa noticed her neighbour looking over at her, out on the porch. The elderly woman's face was distorted with disgust as she shook her head. Jaxon saw his girlfriend's line of sight wasn't on him.

"What's her problem?" He asked.

"I don't know," she said.

Caasa sat on the ground. It was late afternoon,

and most of the villagers were settling down for the day. She was by the staircase below Elder's Hill. She pondered her life with her temple resting on her knee, and her arms wrapped around her legs. Sitting here was her favourite way to relax and unwind, after a rough day of duties for the Council and at home. This peace wouldn't last for long.

"How could you do this to me?!" Kylel asked.

"Excuse me," she said.

"I thought we were going somewhere," he said.

"We're just friends, Jaxon is my boyfriend," she said. She stood up.

"Why have you been leading me on? We were going to fuck," he said.

"I haven't been doing that, I love Jaxon," she said.

"So you're only giving it to him? Fuck me or we're not friends," he said.

Caasa couldn't believe what she was hearing. She was dumbfounded. But she believed she could calm Kylel down.

"I can't and won't sleep with you. I'm sorry you got confused," she said.

She tried to get past Kylel, but he put his arm out to prevent her.

"What do you mean 'can't'?" He asked, smiling gleefully.

"Please, I need to go see Jaxon," she said.

With Kylel's other hand he started touching himself through his pants. Caasa looked wide-eyed, and backed herself against the staircase. He was moaning. She made a break for it, but he hit her on the head, and she stumbled. With her now away from the side of the stairs, he was able to position her how he pleased. He knocked her down onto her back.

"Please... don't," she said.

He paid her pleading no mind. He restrained her wrists above her head with one hand. He removed her clothing with the other hand, so he could see everything he wanted. He parted her legs, and propped them up. He shifted his weight by pinning her to the ground with his hands on her biceps. He took out his penis. He shoved it in. She screamed from the pain, but quickly gave up as she instinctively succumbed to stillness and let her mind wander to anywhere else but here. He continued until he finished... only he wasn't.

He pulled her hair and moved her onto her hands and knees. He wanted to experience her in as many different ways as possible. He wanted to leave his mark. This time, when he was close to finishing, he grabbed her jaw from behind and grunted in her ear.

"You like that don't you, you little slut?" He said. He let go of her face and wiped the hot tears from his hand into his hair. Kylel decided to add variety to his assault; he pulled out his penis, and ejaculated on her back.

Kylel wanted to rape her again, but he was growing tired. He laid down this time. He moved Caasa onto her belly by her hair. When he felt he had a good fistful of it, he raped her mouth and bobbed her head up and down his penis. He came on Caasa's face this time. After raping Caasa three times, he finally fell asleep from the exhaustion.

He rolled over, and she timidly got up and re-dressed. She wiped her face and back. She looked dazed and vacant and was running on instinct. She shuddered her way to Jaxon's parent's place like a scared, wet stray kitten. She sat on his doorstep and hoped he, and only he would notice her. The door opened to Jaxon's mother.

"What are you doing here, you harlot? Get lost," she said.

"Please. Can I see Jaxon?" Caasa asked.

"Honey, who is it?" Jaxon's father asked.

"The trash, sweetie," she said.

Jaxon's father realised what his wife meant and approached the door.

"Get out of here, I won't let you break my son's heart again, you cheating whore," he said.

Caasa's eyes started spilling over from feeling so misunderstood.

"Oh don't give me that look. You were seen flirting with Kylel," the woman said venomously.

Caasa held onto the woman's leg, she didn't want to leave.

"Get off me!" The woman said.

This worked in Caasa's favour. Jaxon came to the front door to investigate.

"I want to talk to her," he said, and Jaxon's parents went inside.

He sat down beside her. He didn't look at her, he couldn't look at her.

"What happened with Kylel?" Jaxon barked.

"Kylel…" She said, her voice breaking at his name. She didn't get any more words out after that.

Jaxon's mother called for him, and he went back inside. His parents still in the kitchen, he entered it, walking lightly. He was expressionless and made no eye contact with either his mother or father.

"Honey, what's the matter? What did *she* do?" His mother asked.

"Kylel hurt her," he said, looking down.

"Yeah, well, she's his problem now," his father said. Jaxon's father implied it was a lover's spat between Caasa and her supposedly new boyfriend.

"No, he *hurt* her," Jaxon corrected.

Jaxon's father processed what his son said. He stood beside him and put a hand on his shoulder.

"You don't want to deal with damaged goods son…" The man said.

"Caasa needs justice," Jaxon said.

"But what about Kylel's future? It would be a shame for this to ruin his life," his mother said.

Jaxon violently shrugged his shoulders and walked away, into his room to pack a bag. He wasn't sure what he needed, but he knew the essentials; some clothes, toiletries, food, blanket and pillow. He would figure the rest out later. He briskly walked past his parents, refusing to make eye contact, out onto the porch and escorted his girlfriend away.

"What are you doing?" Caasa asked.

"We're going to find somewhere to sleep tonight. The sheltered area of the staircase which meets the hill should work," he said.

"No, please no," she was on the verge of hysterics.

Jaxon knew that spot to be his girlfriend's favourite in the village. She went there every day. His eyes widened then softened out of heartbreak.

"Where would you like to go?" He whispered tenderly.

Caasa rotated on the spot, peering in several directions.

"I think I heard the old herbalist's body was found yesterday. There's no one to move in. Maybe there?"

The teenage couple walked to the farthermost point of the pond network to where the herbalist had lived. They took a few wrong turns; it had been years since either of them had been ill, so neither remembered the way there perfectly accurately.

36

When they arrived at the pond it was late at night. It was truly isolated; no one around to disturb them, but neither was there helpful light coming from neighbouring houses. They walked away from the mouth of the cave opening towards the house itself.

There was a faded, dying light on in the work room. Glass shattered around the workbenches and the cauldron had tipped over. The couple looked at each other, realising they had someone; neither could die alone like the herbalist had. They went around to the front door, tentatively in the dark, and attempted to get inside. Jaxon tripped over a bump, which Caasa avoided by shuffling her feet. She felt for an arm to help him up.

Jaxon found a light switch and the house came alive. They waited for their vision to adjust. There were herbalism books open on every table, other modalities too. Cutting boards, knives, pots and pans, wooden spoons, mortar and pestle, herbs hanging to dry, scribbled notes all throughout the house. With the lights now on, they could see the herb gardens through the windows.

The house had been abandoned, but it no longer was. The gardens would perish if they weren't tended to; they had new caretakers and they were willing to learn the craft. The village had lost its herbalist. That was still true. You can't truly care for people who expect you on your knees. You can only truly help people on equal footing, any lesser standing is servitude. Self-sacrifice without consent is exploitation. Over time, the villagers would come to them for healing, but like a caged and prodded animal they could never truly be trusted ever again. For those who knew about Caasa's assault, and treated it as an open secret, they knew that the young couple needed to be kept under watch at all times. That was fine by Caasa and Jaxon. They would also be watching.

Chapter Seven

I aina suppressed the feeling that was trying to float up from her subconscious, and make her question herself. She continued in silence for a little while as she navigated the traditional secret passages of the presiding shaman. Decades ago Iaina had been guided through these underwater caverns and corridors by her mentor. She had been a fully-fledged shaman for nearly twenty years.

As the path to the Tree of Souls went deeper into the underwater labyrinth, the energy began to change. She knew she was getting close when she no longer had to rely on her own biofluorescence to see in the darkness. Finally, she reached the home of all souls, in waiting and dead. The mouth of the cave opened onto a field of seaweed. It swayed in a submerged breeze, a light current revealing that impression. Standing around one hundred feet taller than the seaweed was the tree.

The Tree of Souls glowed with promise. It looked like an old oak, but was translucent and hidden in the depths of an underwater cave system, and protected by that very maze and the consuming darkness.

Iaina walked up to the tree. She sat down in a meditative position and worked on putting herself in the right frame of mind for entering the womb of the tree.

Iaina remained poised in a trance as she stood up and approached the trunk. She cautiously laid her hands upon the main body of the tree to get a sense of how it would react if she walked through it. She felt welcomed by it. It wanted to envelope her in an embrace. She returned the sentiment and stepped forward.

Once inside, an entire reality was laid out before her eyes.

The shaman was greeted by a child, who was a messenger. They stood up to Iaina's hip in height and had the fairer skin of the female-bodied of the species, but made the choice to dress as a boy, wearing baby blue overalls and a wide-brimmed hat. Iaina and the child looked at each other for a few moments, recognising they were alike.

"Hello shaman Iaina. Please follow me. My name is Sythel," said the messenger.

Iaina followed Sythel and did as she was asked. On

the way to wherever the boy was leading her, Iaina admired the architecture. Buildings of irregular shape and colour, like those you would find in a child's drawing; winding paths adorned with glitter, chalk, sequins, puffy bushes; everyone returned to innocence here. Everything bright; there was no darkness here; a land of pure joy, pure expression. All seasons in one day, so that those who preferred winter would get their playtime in the snow and those who favoured summer could do the same in the sand at the beach.

As Iaina ventured deeper into the world of souls, it dawned on her that this was a reversed mirror image of her own. This world is shaped around what the people need, not what is expected of them.

"Where are the adults?" She asked.

"They're here. They don't worry," he said.

"What do you mean?" She asked.

"It's supposed to be a rest after their life," he said.

Iaina went quiet at the realisation she was in the afterlife.

The spirit worker came out from her mind, once she realised she'd left the boy in silence.

"I'm so sorry; I didn't mean to go quiet on you like that," she apologised.

"That's ok. I do the same. I get lost in my mind. My granny says I'm a very curious one. She loves that about me. Maybe she'll like you as much as she does me," he said.

In that instance, Iaina remembered she was talking to a child.

"I don't think your granny loves you because you're curious, I think she loves you because you're her grandson, but thank you anyway," she said.

"You never know, she might. Maybe that's something else we'll have in common," he said.

"Aww... ok, maybe," Iaina relented to his adorableness.

He was a beautiful soul; too pure for her world.

"What are you curious about, Sythel? What do you enjoy?" Iaina asked.

"Um, the world I guess. I love body painting, drawing, helping people and making cookies with my granny or just anything with my granny," Sythel said, beaming.

"Are cookies your favourite food?" The healer asked.

"Yes. Granny says I eat too many and that I won't be able to do that once I'm born. Is that true?" The child asked out of fear.

The fear in Sythel's question, that the idea of not being able to eat cookies for breakfast, lunch and dinner, made the spirit worker chuckle.

"Unfortunately your granny's right. Sorry," Iaina let Sythel down gently.

"Ooh. I don't like it," the boy said, hurt.

"I'm sorry little man. So what do you mean by body painting?" The shaman changed the subject and held in her amusement.

"I love colour, lots of colour. I want to take colour with me everywhere I go," Sythel unbuckled his overalls to show Iaina the sun face he had painted on his torso.

"See. It's the sun, smiling, shining its rays, and it's yellow," he said.

"I like how you've used your skin as the sky, it works really well. It looks nice," she said.

"I thought it made sense, even though we're more purple than blue. I am pale though. I think it's best to use what you have. It would have been too much effort anyway," he admitted.

"Hahaha, that's true… and why not have a purple sky?" She asked.

"Yeah," he said, and did up his overalls.

"How far until we reach our destination?" She asked.

"Not too far. I think you'll like the others," he said.

On the way to the meeting, Sythel took Iaina past the communal kitchen in the park. His grandmother was there.

"Granny! I made a new friend!" Sythel waved at his grandmother while leading Iaina to the meeting.

As Sythel passed his grandmother, Iaina came into view.

"Oh yes, I see dear. That's lovely," Feyea said.

This lovely feeling remained with the shaman for the rest of the way to the meeting.

Iaina and Sythel stood outside the Community Hall where a selection of Council members awaited inside. Iaina admired the blue spiral marble columns which held the frosted glass roof on spikes. This only gave the building its shape. It was really an earthbound treehouse with a muted yellow door, as the rest of the structure was wrapped in vines and surrounded by bushes which were the walls and bore fruit year-round and the trees too.

Sythel too, took a moment to take in the appearance of the delightfully absurd building. He then ran up to the bush to the left of the door and stuck his arm through the green wall and pulled out something Iaina couldn't quite make out. He returned to her side munching on something.

"What are you eating little man?" Iaina asked with amusement.

"Cookies, of course," the mischievous child muffled with a mouth full.

"Sythel! Where are you?" A mystery voice hollered.

"Whoops," Sythel muttered to himself.

The yellow door opened and out stepped a member of the Council. Apparently Sythel had siphoned cookies from a very special cookie hidey hole.

"Sythel, where did you get those cookies?" The Councilwoman asked.

"How do you know these are cookies?" He asked, muffled due to a mouth full of food.

The woman rolled her eyes.

"I'm missing cookies from my stash," Yanay said.

"So? How do you know it was me?" The boy jabbed back.

"I know it's you, because they're all you eat," the Council member announced triumphantly.

Sythel looked down at the ground for a second as if to find his next comeback written down there. He didn't find it.

"Fair," he said.

"And you wanna know something else?" Yanay asked.

"What?" He asked.

"I was near my cookie jar when you stuck your arm through the bush, and I know that's your arm...and you nearly punched me in the stomach when you did that. I had to jump out of the way".

"Shit," he muttered.

"What was that?" Yanay asked.

"Nothing," he said.

The commotion of Yanay's and Sythel's exchange drew the attention of another member of the Council. Iaina recognised him immediately.

"Marl. Is that really you?" Iaina needed confirmation.

"Yes Iaina. It is me. How's my best student been doing?"

"Best student? I was your only student," she said, confused.

"Same thing," Marl said.

"What are you doing here?" Iaina asked, intrigued.

"I died. Remember?" Marl asked.

"Yes Marl. I remember. I was sad to lose a good old friend. So... how have you been? What have you been up to?" Iaina asked.

"Preparing for you, your arrival," he said.

"You... knew I was coming?" She asked.

"Yes. So... you were going to discuss the matter of the village's infertility. Please come inside. Through the door works best," Marl gestured for his former protegee.

"Marl, it can't be," Iaina said in disbelief.

Iaina's phoenix necklace once again seared her.

"Ow," she said.

"I'm afraid that's the nature of what you're dealing with," Marl said.

"How can I fix this...?" She asked.

"Knowing what you know now... Why do you still want to help them?" Marl asked gently.

The necklace now simmered.

Iaina really was going to miss this world and the people she'd met here, especially Sythel. It was uplifting to know that she would return one day, however. Iaina hugged Sythel, then Marl. She was ready to go back. The people of the village had to know the crisis could be solved, if they were willing to change their attitudes and become more accepting. And honestly discuss how power was distributed throughout their society.

The people she had encountered here joined her on her trek back to the door from which she entered, and several more who had heard of her visit followed along too.

Upon approaching the door, she realised she hadn't looked back when she entered this realm. The Tree of Souls looked like a door from this side. Iaina stopped herself before opening the door to look back at her travel party.

"Wow… this has been… a lot…" She said.

"Indeed. I'm sorry to end things on a note like this, but it was good to see you again," Marl said.

Marl and Iaina hugged for the last time. They separated and she looked around once more before leaving this cosy place.

She slowly turned her gaze around to capture the faces of the people giving her, her send off. Sythel with his grandmother Feyea, her mentor Marl, the Councilwoman Yanay, many others too; she then saw a little figure peeping from behind a pair of legs which belonged to a young woman in her twenties, their caretaker most likely.

The figure appeared to look on at Iaina with wonder, as they forgot their shyness and stood out a little farther and draped their caretaker's leg. It was then that Iaina realised the small figure had a deep skin tone and was dressed in the frilliest dress she had ever seen.

The shaman embraced the admiring girl with her eyes and a warm smile. The feeling of a shared reality was apparent even though the little girl looked to be about four. Iaina enjoyed this blip in time, but it wasn't long before she felt a sense of self-pity and mourning fall over her as her gaze turned upwards towards the girl's caretaker, who was stroking her hair. She had never had that. This is what she would fight for.

She stepped through the door without hesitation.

8

Chapter Eight

Iaina stepped back into her world, out of the Tree of Souls... how was she going to do this?

The shaman sat down again before the Tree of Souls, this time facing away from it and towards the entrance to the cave, and by extension towards the village. Her mind, body and soul were in unison in their determination to reach the village. With Iaina being this fired up, she accessed the state necessary to telepathically communicate with the Council easier than she ever had before. Once done, she leapt up from her seated position and practically ran in the dark, through the underwater cave system back to her home.

Iaina walked up the steps out of a pond which resided below Elders Hill. Around her, people from the village were giving her filthy looks as they did the same as her from similar ponds. She went the same way as them to the top of the hill, but kept going and went inside to find a member of the Council to announce her presence. She figured there would be a few thousand people gathered outside by the time she came back out. It didn't matter how many people there would be.

Inside she found, of all people, Lithinel and Kylel. Seeing these two men, she knew she needed to remember her task. This worked to calm her.

"I have the answer. Allow me to speak," she said.

"What is the solution, shaman?" Lithinel asked in his booming chest voice.

"Please. I must deliver the news as soon as possible, Councilman," Iaina mirrored his tone.

"You will not be speaking. I will be. We don't need you influencing people. What is the solution?" Her former friend demanded the answer.

Iaina didn't feel it was likely for Lithinel to accept what she had to say... but she couldn't just announce the way out of the infertility problem without his permission. He, and very likely his despicable son, would use force to silence her.

Iaina feigned the appearance of defeat by slowly turning around and walking out with slumped shoulders. Just before leaving the Council chambers, and while unknowingly still in sight of the father and son pair, she bolted out onto the clearing at the top of the hill where the crowd was gathered. As

Lithinel and Kylel had seen her do this, they gave chase.

She stepped onto a little platform, above the crowd. She spoke.

"Listen. I know the answer. The reason you're not able to conceive is your future children are refusing to be born," she said.

"What do you mean?" One man asked.

"They all despise your society. They would loathe to live amongst you and see how you treat some people as different, while others you treat as disposable. or you silence them, ignore their pain. Judge their decisions, when you have no clue what they're going through. They have no intention of letting these things continue and need you to change, for you to start having children again," she said.

The crowd couldn't contain its disgust.

But instead of acting on this new mood of theirs, it seemed as though they had become deferential towards her. Iaina was mistaken. Lithinel had come into view.

Lithinel stepped forward with a triumphant, gloating look in his eyes. They were thin like needles and his aura reeked of arrogance pungent enough to incapacitate a fish like the one Iaina summoned. He tried to shoo her.

"So nice of you to finally show," Lithinel said, as he took control of the crowd.

"What you have suggested is preposterous. Leave before I make you regret coming here," he said.

At the implication of physical violence, the crowd transformed into a mob. It had never really been safe for Iaina there, but now it was apparent.

Men standing just beneath the platform reached up to grab her skirts, to lift them and teach her a lesson. As one of them nearly had a hold of her, Kylel was coming up from behind to pin her arms behind her back and bend her over. All the people there wanted to make their feelings for Iaina's very existence known. She disgusted them.

None of them would get their most desired opportunity, to rid the world of Iaina's perceived degeneracy.

Iaina lifted herself three feet into the air. She was untouchable now. Stiffened, she was ready for travel. She glided through the air. She dropped down into the pond she came from, a few seconds after leaving the grasp of the incited mob. She couldn't bring herself to move.

She laid in the foetal position at the bottom of the stairs. The phoenix necklace scorched her neck this time. She writhed in pain.

"Ok, I get it!" She said.

Her yelling acted like a beacon to the incessant horde. The group, led by Kylel, descended the stairs of the pond Iaina was soothing herself in. She startled, but not soon enough.

Kylel moved her onto her back, leaving her completely defenceless and open to attack. For old time's sake, he grabbed her by the throat, but this was not how he had chose to end her life. He wanted his fun with her first. Kylel ordered the men he brought with him to hold down her limbs. They had her pinned instantly.

With a man on each of her arms and legs, and Kylel hovered over her torso, at her neck, the group of men begin to carry out their plan for her. The men on Iaina's limbs take out their knives, ready to run them through her hands and feet. Once truly pinned, like a five-pointed star, Kylel plans on finishing what he started back in her home.

The man on Iaina's left arm slides his knife into her hand with glee. She is brought back to reality by the resonance of her own scream.

"AAAHHHHH!" She said.

"That's good. That's what we want. How about you stick it in his foot, yeah?" Kylel asked, pleased.

Iaina whimpered; from the existing pain and from the fear of what was to come.

The man in charge of the spirit worker's right foot had his turn. He slid his knife in like the other had. Iaina reacted as expected.

"AAAAAHHHHH! Please stop... please... I'm begging you... just leave me alone... I won't bother you anymore," Iaina said.

"Too late for that," said the man who just put a knife in the shaman's right foot.

Kylel decided to reveal his plan for Iaina.

"Do you know what I'm going to do to you, you disgusting freak?" He said.

"No. Please let me go," Iaina said through tears and mucous.

"Ha. No. I'm going to pin you like a starfish, then I'm going to cut it off. When I get sick of watching you bleed out, I'm going to plunge this knife in your fucking throat. Do you understand?" Kylel laid out.

"Please... don't," Iaina said, sobbing.

Before the men could get any farther with their vile designs, a shadow from the deep, arrived. No time was wasted in disposing of the scum.

At the appearance of the ominous shadow, the men had stood up to peer at it. This was one of their many mistakes. Being born was another; they would come to regret it.

The fish went for the man on Iaina's left hand first. It bit off his left arm; sweet revenge. The man continued to cry and scream, to no avail. This started what would become a bloodbath. The fish with the jaw power of the fiercest predators, moved from his left arm to his right. Spitting them both out. The other men tried running for their lives, up the stairs; so very pointless.

Next, it had a chomp on one of the men's legs. It spat that out too. Then, for a bit of good fun it engulfed the man up to the waist and crushed his ribs and squeezed out his organs and eyes. He was now in several pieces and very dead.

The fish continued to do Iaina's bidding. All of them got bitten in half at the waist and spat out. Iaina could hear the screams. Her sight was obscured by the blood from all the carnage the fish was wreaking. Kylel was last, no one was going to save him; the same fear Iaina had had twice now at the hands of Kylel. There was no gargantuan creature coming to his aid. She was the one who could summon animals.

Iaina wouldn't know quite what had happened... because she left. She left in a shower of body parts. She maintained her sense of will and purpose, fought the desire to pass out from the blood loss and pain, and pulled the knives out with her free hand. Resisting her body and soul compelling her to collapse, she crawled away from the village, to where, she wasn't sure. Sometimes she was on her hands and knees, other times she was dragging herself against the ground on her belly. She would have to wait for the delirium to subside to figure out where she was.

9

Chapter Nine

"Euuuggghhh," Iaina woke up feeling ill from swaying.

She had been found by a couple and carried inside to their house. They had cleaned and bandaged her wounds. She awoke on a bench. She was on edge and startled, and looked around for a way out.

"Calm down," Caasa said.

The woman thought to pin Iaina down, but stopped herself. She wasn't an idiot and had figured out how Iaina got the knife marks in her hands and feet. Pinning Iaina would only farther traumatise her.

Iaina looked around and realised she had been here before, recently too. Her gaze settled on a woman.

"Caasa," Iaina said.

The man who had carried Iaina in looked between

the two women.

"Do you two know each other?" Jaxon asked.

"Sort of, she came around and asked some questions about the infertility," Caasa said.

Jaxon nodded. He thought he was just helping *the shaman*, he didn't know they were on first-name basis.

"So you're on a first-name basis?" Jaxon asked.

"Um... no, actually. I never got your name," Caasa said.

"Iaina," Iaina said.

Jaxon rolled his eyes. His wife had never been particularly good at getting to know people. The amount of times she would *describe* a person they had treated, but couldn't *name* them. A patient was a patient to her.

Iaina realised the opportune moment to avoid having this exchange again.

"And your name was...?" Iaina asked.

"Oh, Jaxon. Sorry," Jaxon chuckled.

"Great. Now that we all know each other, let's get to the critical matter. What the hell happened?" Caasa asked.

Iaina propped herself up on the bench with her elbows and rolled her head back. She sighed heavily and lifted her head back up. Iaina started tracing random shapes on the bench with a finger. She was figuring out how to articulate what happened.

"I told the village something they didn't want to hear... and I was gifted with knives... in my hands and feet," Iaina said.

"Sounds like a normal Tuesday," Caasa nodded slowly.

Jaxon stood there holding his shaking head in his hands. He looked up.

"Would you two be serious please," Jaxon said.

The women shared a smirk. Caasa cleared her throat.

"So what did you tell them?" Caasa asked.

"The total infertility is because the souls of future children are refusing to be born. I gave them an ultimatum. Change or death. They chose death," Iaina said.

"What would they have to change?" Caasa asked.

"Society. Its structure, how it works, who it benefits," Iaina said.

"At least they won't be after you now," Jaxon said.

Iaina thought that was a complicated matter.

"In getting away..." Iaina said.

She paused for a moment on how to deliver this delicately. She didn't know how this would be received.

"Kylel's dead," Iaina said.

Caasa had a thousand yard stare. Jaxon looked over at his wife. Iaina noticed Jaxon's line of sight was fixed on Caasa.

"Are you alright?" Iaina asked.

"I'll be fine, thank you," Caasa said. Her blinking returned to normal and she nodded slightly. She had a soft, peaceful smile now.

"Is it ok if I wait here until it's dark enough for me to sneak back to my shack?" Iaina asked.

"Yeah that's fine," Caasa said. Jaxon nodded.

Once Iaina thought it would be easier to hide from the patrolling lynch mobs, she left the seclusion of Caasa and Jaxon's house and the outermost pond. She made it out of the network of ponds by jumping fences and vaulting over seaweed hedges as need be. She nearly got back to her shack completely unnoticed, but at the entrance to her pond stood someone waiting for her.

"Zirr," Iaina said.

"Come with me. I want to show you something," Zirr said.

"I haven't been completely honest with you, but I wasn't protecting myself," Zirr said.

Iaina screwed her face up in confusion.

"Just follow me," Zirr said.

Zirr took Iaina to where he really lived. They had only ever met on the top of a hill secluded from the village, under what used to be stars, but were clearly now the eyes of a phoenix burning into them. To the two shamans, at least, and maybe a handful of others.

The excuse he had given before for not showing her where he lived, was that he was a wanderer and came and went as he pleased. Which wasn't a complete lie. He had wandered... but then he had found.

Zirr led Iaina into a canyon from a flat grassy area, through a passageway of rocky outcroppings, down a hill to a stony riverbed with patches of lush greenery by a river. A waterfall fed the river. In all, it was an idyllic paradise.

"Where I came from, has been through the same thing the village you swore to serve is going through right now," Zirr said.

"I had to walk away. I couldn't change them," Zirr said.

He held in bursting into tears. He breathed deeply, composing himself. Iaina looked at him with concern. He had never done that in all the years she had known him. He cleared his throat.

"Then I got curious and went looking for others. I found some," Zirr said. He had a glint of hope in his eyes.

"I didn't tell you this because they didn't want to be bothered by anyone. We found our little paradise here... and we're just living out the rest of our days... " Zirr said.

"Can I see them?" Iaina asked.

"They're asleep by the fire, behind the waterfall," Zirr said.

Zirr led her along the riverbed to a short set of terraced steps. She climbed them and gazed upon the group. The necklace let Iaina know of its presence without hurting her. There were around two dozen people, but five different races not including Zirr.

That's all the people he could find... from the villages that were dying out. Eventually, their species would be extinct.

10

Chapter Ten

Iaina stood beside the Tree of Souls, admiring it in a trance. The only thing snapping her out of it was the pain in her neck from craning it in this position. She was brought back to the task at hand at the searing sensation. She had telepathically sent directions to Lithinel, so he could meet her at the Tree of Souls. If this went well, Iaina's final tactic would work. Extinction wasn't what she wanted… but she was prepared for it.

Lithinel appeared around the corner from the entrance of the cave. He disappeared into the seaweed meadow for a few moments before reappearing.

"Are you ready for what I'm about to show you?" Iaina asked.

Lithinel gestured for Iaina to continue.

"The tree behind me is how I discovered the souls of the unborn, the pre-born, are refusing to enter this world, and inhabit a body in your society. That's where the souls are," Iaina said. Iaina turned to her side to look at the tree, and look at Lithinel.

Lithinel took the tree in slowly. He was willing and listening. He looked attentive. He returned his gaze to his old friend.

"It's also the afterlife. I've met some people there, that I knew from the village," Iaina said. She glanced back.

Lithinel's eyebrows raised for a second and he compressed his lips. Or so Iaina thought. She wasn't sure what she saw out of the corner of her eye.

Lithinel walked past Iaina and put his hands on the tree.

"So extraordinary. Beautiful," Lithinel said.

"You can feel the aliveness of the tree, can't you?" Iaina asked.

Lithinel clawed at the energy emanating from the tree. He was trying to break in.

"Give me my son back!" Lithinel demanded.

It didn't matter that he had only gripped at the energy emanating from the tree, his action had still triggered a defensive response.

Something Iaina had not conceived as possible, nor Lithinel, had considered as a consequence, happened. The branches of the tree came alive and wrapped themselves around Lithinel's neck in an effort to strangle the invading force into submission. The tree used Lithinel's immobility from the counterattack to great effect. It slipped some of its branches down his body, and in doing so crushed and exploded him. He was eradicated in a blood splatter that quickly lost shape in the current of the water.

Iaina stood there with a wide-eyed blank look on her face, slowly running her fingers through her hair to remove the remains. The phoenix fell from her neck, sinking down like lead to the pond floor, and combusted. She watched it, nodding, as it turned to ashes before her eyes.

The unofficial leader of the village, the uncrowned king had abdicated his throne. The man who could have been the Voice of Reason for the village, just lost his head... and got himself killed.

You're all fucked... your heads are in your asses.

And Iaina walked away. She chose death.

Epilogue

The Tree of Souls stirred for the first time in decades. Ethereal light returned, and hummed from the branches and trunk. The tree no longer appeared to be dead. The home of all worthy souls began to crack open, and shed its armaments of hardened offshoots, shielding bark and striking, piercing branches that were the artillery that had slain those who dared to mark it. From the once oft-traversed gateway, came a voice; the last voice to utter a sound before being sealed away into the afterlife.

"Please be careful. I know you will be, and that you can handle yourself, and take care of yourself... but you've never been outside of the tree. Please be careful," Iaina spoke.

"Jeez Mum... you trained me to be a shaman. I can handle anything that comes my way," Iaina's son said.

"I know Iainan... I just... still remember how nasty of a place the physical world was," Iaina said.

Iainan softened at his mother's worry. He kissed her on the cheek and held her in a reassuring hug.

He broke the hug and placed his hands on either of Iaina's shoulders.

"Would you like to come with me? To make sure I'm safe," Iainan said.

"No, you'll be ok," Iaina said.

"I love you Mum," Iainan said.

"I love you too. I guess you should probably get going, so you don't give Mama, Uncle Jaxon or your brothers and sisters a chance to restrain you, and stop you from leaving," Iaina said.

"Yeah, I guess you did tell them you would handle it, being the other shaman in the family," Iainan said.

With that, Iainan stepped outside of the Tree of Souls.

He stood upon earthly ground… and felt different. Even though his parents had entered the tree alive, and he was born like you or I, it was still odd how tangible this world was. Then he looked up, and had his first learning experience of this world.

"Whoa. Check out all these people here," Iainan said.

"Those are ghosts, sweetie. They can't make it in. Actually, that is a lot of them. I didn't realise how many there would be. Has it really been that long?" Iaina said.

Iainan waited for the conclusion to his mother's audible train of thought. He zoned out for the briefest of moments, and then heard an uptick in pitch. This piqued his attention.

"You know what sweetie? If there are that many ghosts, it's probably really safe for you to travel on your own. The people you encounter, if they aren't dead, they'll be too old and decrepit to hurt you. Go for it, it'll be great," she said.

"Yes Mum," Iainan said.

The son of Iaina and Caasa weaved his way through the seaweed meadow, pausing to admire it's likeness to his mother's and uncle's descriptions. It was the same height he had gotten the impression it was; it wasn't consuming the cavern, for everything was in balance here, it was natural. It hadn't just kept growing. He caught sight of a glimmering light from the corner of his eye. It was the tree.

"Is that what you look like? I came out of that," Iainan said.

Glowing, swaying; the Tree of Souls was even stranger yet more captivating than he had pictured. Taking in everything available to his senses, an otherworldly tranquillity came over the young man. He decided to hold onto this lovely, yet unfortunately rare feeling for the rest of his walk to the village his parents once called home. That's where he headed.

He enjoyed the stroll through the corridors with the occasional lighting, but it was mostly dark.

Finally, he got to the village. It smelt of decay. It was desolate, and eerily quiet, but not completely.

But he could hear moaning, agony moaning. He moved in on the location of the sound. It felt uncomfortable, but he entered a house that wasn't his. He rounded the corner to what looked to be a bedroom, and inside he saw a very old man having a heart attack. Iainan witnessed death for the first time in his life. Where he was born, there had been no death; this sight rattled him.

Despite this horror, this unfamiliarity, he approached the dying man. The man's eyes locked onto him out of desperation, anguish and fear. Right as Iainan stood beside him, in his bed, the man grabbed him. Though startled, Iainan offered his abilities.

"I'm a shaman, I can ease your transition to the next life," Iainan said.

"You're a shaman? You... better not... be like... that bastard... or the other two worthless shits," the fading man said.

With that statement, the dying man lost the help and support of the shaman. Iainan walked away and left that man to his agony. Before he had disappeared from the room, the man called out.

"So you are?!" He croaked.

"Only when you insult my family," Iainan said without looking back.

He reneged on his original decision. He stood there and watched the bigoted, hateful man die. Iainan figured it would be good for him to become accustomed to death; he was to see this man become a ghost. Now to start roaming, raving, hungering and languishing. He stayed until it was done.

Iainan had seen enough. His mother's and uncle's decisions now resonated with him; he too would abandon the village and leave it to its devices. You can't genuinely help people who expect it of you.

The first-time traveller imagined what the homes of his parents were like. He remembered some of the details given to him by Mum, Mama and Uncle Jaxon. He ventured farther into the labyrinth of ponds till he came upon Caasa and Jaxon's tiny, isolated, and now derelict dwelling.

It looked like it had been abandoned, in a rush, and indeed it had. The water of the pond somehow seemed stagnant, though it was connected to all the others. Iainan felt the urge to go through his mother's things to salvage what there was of her life before him, but realised it was unnecessary. Jaxon and Caasa's pond had remained undisturbed since then; this was the perfect resting place, a memorial for her from before the upheaval.

There was only one place left to check out in the immediate area; Mum's place, Iaina's shack. He relived the experience he had had at Mama and Uncle Jaxon's place.

Then Iainan trekked all the way back through the ponds, but diverged from the path by continuing on his way to the staircase below Elders Hill. He stood at the bottom of the steps, and recalled the terrible things done to his mother's here. He wouldn't have been born if those men had succeeded. He steeled himself, inhaled, and made the ascent.

This was his first time standing on dry land in the world of the living. He felt the grass between his toes. He had done this multiple times on the other side; what struck him wasn't how different this world was, but how similar, at least in schema.

Iainan turned around as he noticed a throng of wandering spirits in the water, going from door to door seeking assistance, finding no one. He became so engrossed by this spectacle he didn't see this coming. A different old man than before, lunged from the top step and clung to Iainan's leg, frantic for assistance.

"Please, for the love of everything that is good... help me," he cried.

Iainan didn't know what to make of this display. He had resigned himself as a traveller, not as a healer; he concluded it wasn't really possible to help the surviving villagers. Who said he was obligated, anyway? What if letting in the souls of those who roam the world, ruins the sanctuary of the afterlife? What if they recreate the world of the living there? What if the tree revolts?

"I'm sorry, I don't think I can help you," Iainan

said.

And he walked off, through a grassy open field, he disappeared. He never would return to the tree. There was too much exploration to do; his head too full of stories to go back to the comfort he hadn't earned. Iainan found the physical world much more enchanting than the world he had been born into. This irony his mothers and uncles had seen coming, but for him it had only lurked as a half-thought beneath the surface. Still, they thought he would come home someday. But even in death he wouldn't.

He rambled all over the world for the next sixty odd years, living off the lands and lakes, requesting the creatures to give themselves up to him as sustenance, and transport, and it being granted. On occasion he would aid roving ghosts to move on to their ultimate lodging; sweet respite was theirs at last. And over the course of these decades, Iainan always maintained hope at the prospect of finding the real, last stragglers, who Uncle Zirr hadn't managed to gather. This could not have gone on indefinitely however. When it finally came time for his own passing, he chose to stay back, and in spirit, guide the evolution of the species he encountered to humanoid consciousness. He had transcended the limitations of a living or dead shaman; he had become godlike.

Iainan, son of Iaina and Caasa, passer of thresholds, was now steward to all life on this verdant, blooming planet. The next cycle of life begins. Let's hope this one isn't fucked all up.

www.ingramcontent.com/pod-product-compliance
Lightning Source LLC
Chambersburg PA
CBHW030418120726
47904CB00007B/2327